The Little Prince

READ-ALOUD STORYBOOK

based on the masterpiece by Antoine de Saint-Exupéry

HOUGHTON MIFFLIN HARCOURT

Boston   New York

When I was six I gave up my magnificent career as an artist. I had to choose another profession, so I learned how to fly a plane. I lived all alone, without anyone I could really talk to, until six years ago when I made a crash landing in the Sahara Desert. Something had gone wrong with the plane's engine. On the first night, I fell asleep on the sand, a thousand miles from the nearest civilization. So you can imagine my surprise when, at sunrise, a funny little voice woke me up saying:

"Please . . . draw me a sheep."

"Huh?"

"Draw me a sheep . . ."

I leapt to my feet as if I'd been struck by lightning. I rubbed my eyes. And I saw the most extraordinary little man standing there, examining me from head to toe. I told him (I was quite annoyed) that I didn't know how to draw. He answered:

"It doesn't matter. Draw me a sheep."

So I started to draw. He watched me closely. Then he said, "No, that one is already very sick. Draw another one."

I started to draw again. My friend smiled kindly. He said, "That's not a sheep; it's a ram. It has horns . . ."

So I scrawled out one last drawing. "This is a crate," I said. "The sheep you want is inside the crate." I was quite surprised when I saw my young judge's face light up.

"That's just what I wanted! But do you think a sheep like this needs a lot of grass? Because where I come from, everything is really small."

And that's how I first met the little prince. But it wasn't until much later that I finally understood where he had come from.

I learned something very important: the planet he came from was barely bigger than a house! The little prince asked, "It's true, isn't it, that sheep eat bushes?"

"Yes, that's right."

"Oh, that's good. So they must eat baobabs, too, right?"

Because, you see, there were some terrible seeds on the little prince's planet . . . baobab seeds. The planet's soil was full of them. Now, with a baobab, if you allow it to grow too much, you can never get rid of it again. It will take over the whole planet. It will riddle the planet with roots. And if the planet is too small, and if there are too many baobabs, the planet will explode.

The little prince pressed me with questions. "If a sheep eats bushes, does it eat flowers, too?"

"A sheep eats everything it finds."

"Even flowers that have thorns?"

"Yes, even flowers that have thorns."

"Then what's the point of having thorns?"

"There isn't any point. It's pure meanness on the part of the flower!"

After a brief silence he burst out, rather grudgingly: "I don't believe you! What if I know of a flower that is unique, a flower that doesn't exist anywhere else except on my planet?"

And with that he began to cry. I held him in my arms until he fell asleep.

It wasn't long before I heard all about this flower. It had sprouted one day from a seed that appeared out of nowhere. The little prince had kept a close watch on this tiny sprig that didn't look like any other sprig. The flower took ages and ages to bloom, to come out of its little green shelter of a bud. It took its time deciding what color to be. It dressed itself slowly, deliberately, adjusting its petals one by one. It didn't want petals all rumpled, like those of a poppy. Oh, no. This was a very stylish flower! And then suddenly one morning, there she was!

"Ah, here I am," the little blossom said. "I'm barely awake . . . I'm still all disheveled . . ."

But the little prince couldn't contain his admiration: "How lovely you are!" he said.

It wasn't long before the flower began to torment him with her vanity. One day the flower said to the little prince: "I'm terrified of drafts. You don't happen to have a shelter, do you?"

"Terrified of drafts, are you? . . . That's not a very good thing for a plant, is it?" remarked the little prince. "Quite a complicated flower . . ."

"At night I want you to put me under a glass cover. It's very cold here where you live." And, to make sure the little prince had gotten the point, the flower coughed two or three times. So, despite his growing affection, the little prince began to grow unhappy.

To escape his sadness, it seems, the little prince hitched a ride with a wild flock of migrating birds. He traveled through the region of asteroids 325, 326, 327 . . .

So, he began to visit them. The first one was inhabited by a king. But the little prince was astonished—the planet was so tiny that he wondered what ever could the king rule over?

"Over everything," the king answered simply. With a vague wave of his hand, the king pointed out his planet, the other planets, and all the stars.

"And the stars, too, obey you?"

"Of course," the king answered. "They, too, obey. I don't tolerate disobedience." The little prince was impressed by such a show of power. He said boldly: "I'd like to see a sunset . . . Can you command the sun to set?"

"You'll have your sunset," answered the king. "I'll command it. It will be tonight around . . . around . . . around seven forty! Then you'll see how my commands are obeyed."

The second planet was inhabited by a very vain man: "Ah-ha! Here comes an admirer!" cried the vain man from a distance, as soon as he saw the little prince. Because, you see, to vain people, all other people are admirers.

"Don't you just admire me to no end?" he asked the little prince.

"What does *admire* mean?" asked the little prince.

"To *admire* means to acknowledge that I am the most handsome, the best dressed, the richest, and the most intelligent person on the planet."

"But you're the *only* person on your planet!"

And the little prince left. "Grownups are so strange," he said to himself as he went on his way.

The next planet belonged to a businessman. He was so busy that he didn't even look up when the little prince arrived.

"Three and two make five. Hello. Twenty-two and six, twenty-eight. Wow! That's five hundred and one million, six hundred twenty-two thousand, seven hundred and thirty-one."

"Five hundred million what?"

"Millions of those tiny things one sometimes sees in the sky."

"Do you mean flies?"

"No, not those. The little glistening gold things that make lazy people daydream."

"Oh, you mean stars. And what do you do with five hundred million stars?"

"Nothing. I just own them."

"But what do you do with them?"

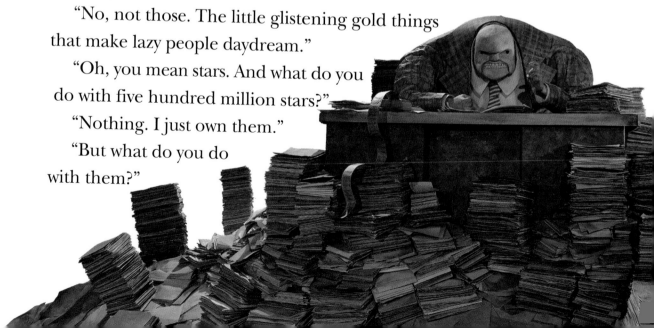

"I count them and then count them again," the businessman said.

"I own a flower that I water every day," the little prince told him. "And it's a good thing for my flower that I own her. But you, you're not that useful to the stars . . ."

And he went on his way.

Once he'd reached Earth, the little prince was quite surprised not to see anyone. After a long walk across deserts, rocks, and tracts of snow, he discovered a garden of blossoming roses.

"Good morning," said the roses.

The little prince gazed at them. They all looked just like his flower. He felt very sad. His flower had told him she was the only one of her kind in the whole universe. And here were five thousand of them, all exactly the same, in just one garden!

And he lay down on the grass and wept.

That is when the fox appeared.

"Good morning. I'm over here," said a voice, "under the apple tree . . ."

"Who are you?" asked the little prince. "You're very handsome."

"I'm a fox," said the fox.

"Come play with me," the little prince suggested. "I'm so sad . . ."

"I can't play with you," the fox said. "I'm not tamed."

"Oh, excuse me," said the little prince. "What does *tamed* mean?"

"It means 'to create ties with,'" the fox answered. "To me, right now, you're just a little boy, no different from a hundred thousand other little boys. And I don't need you. And you don't need me, either. I'm nothing to you but a fox like any other hundred thousand foxes. But if you tame me, we'll need each other.

"You'll be the only boy in the world for me. I'll be the only fox in the world for you."

"I'm beginning to understand," the little prince said. "There's this flower . . . I think she has tamed me . . ."

If you tame me," the fox said, "my life will be filled with sunshine. Look at the fields of wheat. I don't eat bread. To me, wheat is useless. But your hair is the color of gold. So it will be marvelous once you've tamed me. The wheat, which is golden, will remind me of you . . ."

The fox fell silent and stared at the little prince for a long time:

"Please, tame me!" he said.

"I'd like to," the little prince answered. "What do I have to do?"

"You have to be patient," the fox answered. "First, sit down at a little distance from me, like this, on the grass. I'll watch you out of the corner of my eye, and you won't say anything. Words often lead to misunderstandings. Then, each day, you can sit a little closer to me . . ."

The next day the little prince came back.

"It would have been better if you'd come back at the same time," the fox said. "If, for example, you come at four o'clock in the afternoon, by three o'clock I'll start feeling happy. The closer it gets to four o'clock, the happier I'll be. But if you come at any old time, I'll never know when to prepare my heart for rejoicing . . ."

So the little prince tamed the fox.

And then it was time to leave. "You look like you're going to cry!" said the little prince.

"Yes, of course," the fox said.

"Then what's the point?"

"The point," said the fox, "is the color of the wheat. That's my secret. It's very simple: One sees clearly only with the heart. Anything that is important is invisible to the eye."

"Anything that is important," the little prince repeated so that he wouldn't forget it, "is invisible to the eye."

"It's all the time you've spent on your rose that makes your rose so important," the fox said. "Once you've tamed something, you're responsible for it forever. You are responsible for your rose."

By now it was the eighth day after my crash landing in the desert, and I'd listened to this story as I drank the last drop of my water supply. So we started walking. When we'd walked for hours, night fell and the stars began to appear. The little prince said, "The stars are beautiful because of a flower we can't see, and what's beautiful about the desert is that it's hiding a well somewhere we can't see . . ." As the little prince was falling asleep, I picked him up and started out again. I found the well at daybreak. I lifted the pail up to his lips. He drank from it, eyes closed.

"Where you're from," said the little prince, "people plant five thousand roses in a single garden . . . but they don't find what they are looking for . . . and yet, what they're looking for can be found in a single rose, or in a sip of water . . . but the eyes are blind. You have to search with your heart."

Beside the well there was the ruin of an old stone wall. The next day, I saw my little prince, from a distance, sitting up on it, his legs dangling. And I heard him say to someone:

"Do you have some good venom? Are you sure you won't make me suffer a long time?"

So I bounded over! It was one of those snakes that can kill you in thirty seconds. I reached the wall just in time to catch my good little prince, pale as snow, in my arms. He said:

"I'm going home today . . . I've got your sheep. And I've got its crate. Tonight will mark one year. My star will be exactly above the place where I fell last year . . . I'm going to give you a gift . . . Because I live on one of the stars, and will be laughing up there on one of them, whenever you look up at the sky at night, to you it will seem as if all the stars are laughing. You will have stars that know how to laugh. It will be as if, instead of stars, I'd given you a whole lot of little bells that know how to laugh . . . "

I'm sure he got back to his planet, because at daybreak I couldn't find him anywhere around. And at night, I love listening to the stars. It's like five hundred million bells . . .